GATOR
ON MY
BACK

Written and illustrated
by
Mary Ann Burrows

◆ FriesenPress

Suite 300 - 990 Fort St
Victoria, BC, V8V 3K2
Canada

www.friesenpress.com

ISBN
978-1-5255-7035-3 (Hardcover)
978-1-5255-7036-0 (Paperback)
978-1-5255-7037-7 (eBook)

1. JUVENILE FICTION, SOCIAL ISSUES, DEPRESSION & MENTAL ILLNESS

Distributed to the trade by The Ingram Book Company

Dedicated to everyone who has ever had
an alligator on their back.

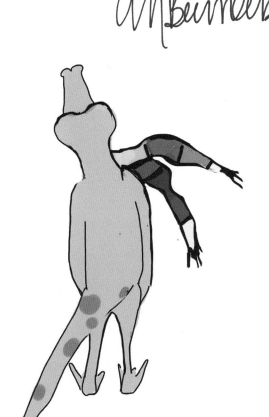

One day a slimy alligator climbed onto a boy's back.

It turned his
happy into sad
and turned his
light to black.

The boy's heart felt very heavy,
his head faced to the ground.

His eyes looked sad and empty,
his smile turned to a frown.

He gathered up his favorite things
and put them in a pack.
He set out to find a better place, and said,

"I WON'T BE BACK!"

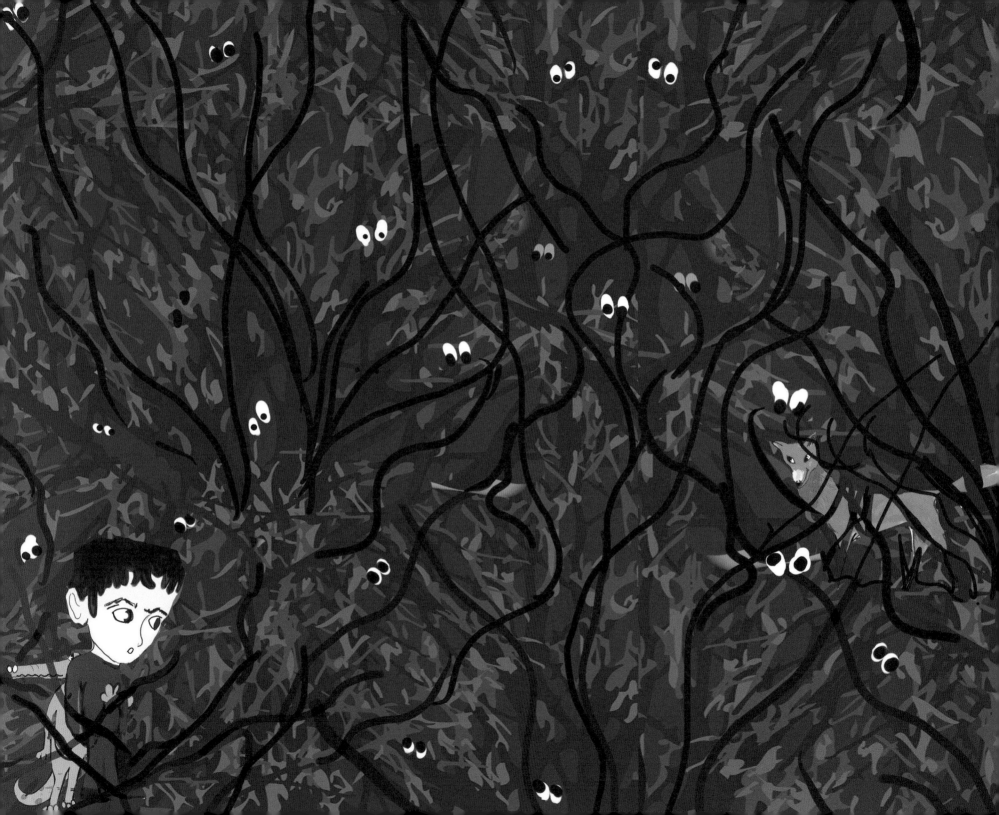

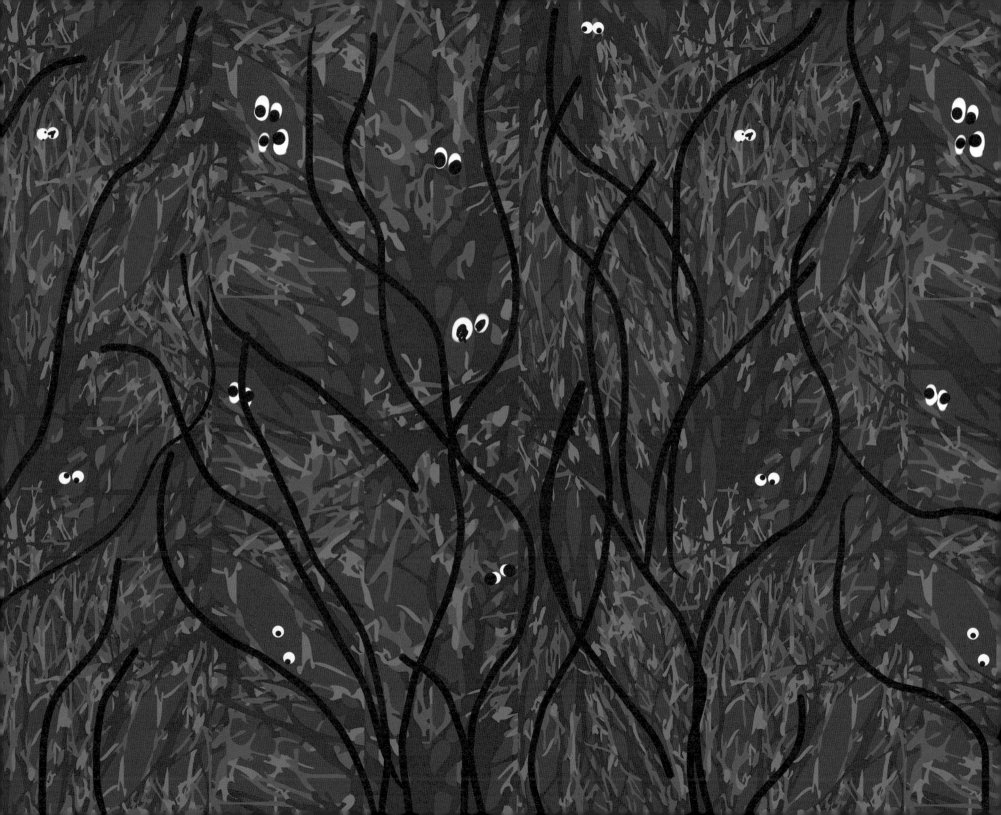

The boy talked about his feelings.

Gator **FELT AFRAID.**

He jumped off the pack, ran away, and hid inside a cave.

The boy walked on. His pack felt light,
and he soon began to see
that he was fine without his friend,

in fact,
he now
FELT FREE.

While on his own, the boy felt strong.

He felt like he could fly.

He sang with birds, he made a fort,

took photos of the sky.

The boy soon saw the Gator's thoughts
had taken quite a hold.

He had to get his own mind back,
and needed to take control.

Gator crawled out of the cave
and climbed upon the pack.

"HANG ON!"
yelled the boy

"Let's set some rules,
before you can come back!"

"I'm in charge, that's number one,
and I am not your clown.

I accept that you're a part of me but
GEEZ you weigh me down.

I want to smile.

I want to laugh.

I want to have more friends.

All your talk about me being bad,
Gator, it has to end!"

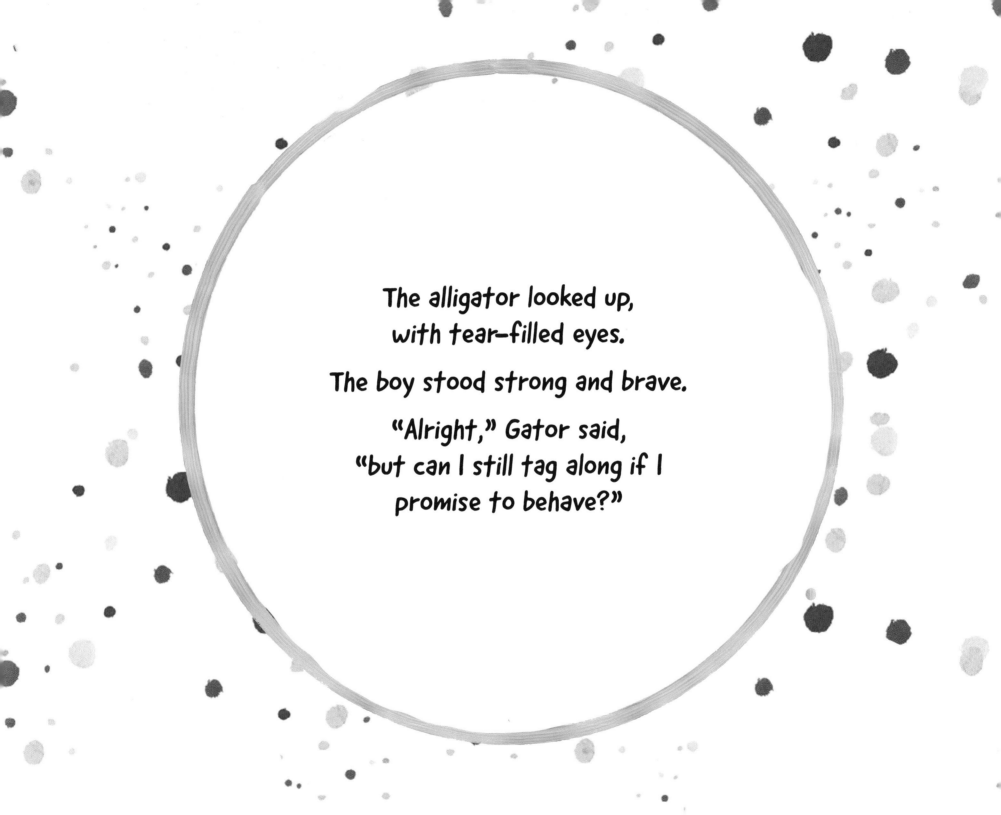

The alligator looked up,
with tear-filled eyes.

The boy stood strong and brave.

"Alright," Gator said,
"but can I still tag along if I
promise to behave?"

So off they went on through the world with a whole new set of rules.

Gator knew that the boy was in charge and his power had been

DIFFUSED.

From that day on the alligator was pretty well behaved.

But once in a while, when he forgets, the boy sends him back to his cave.

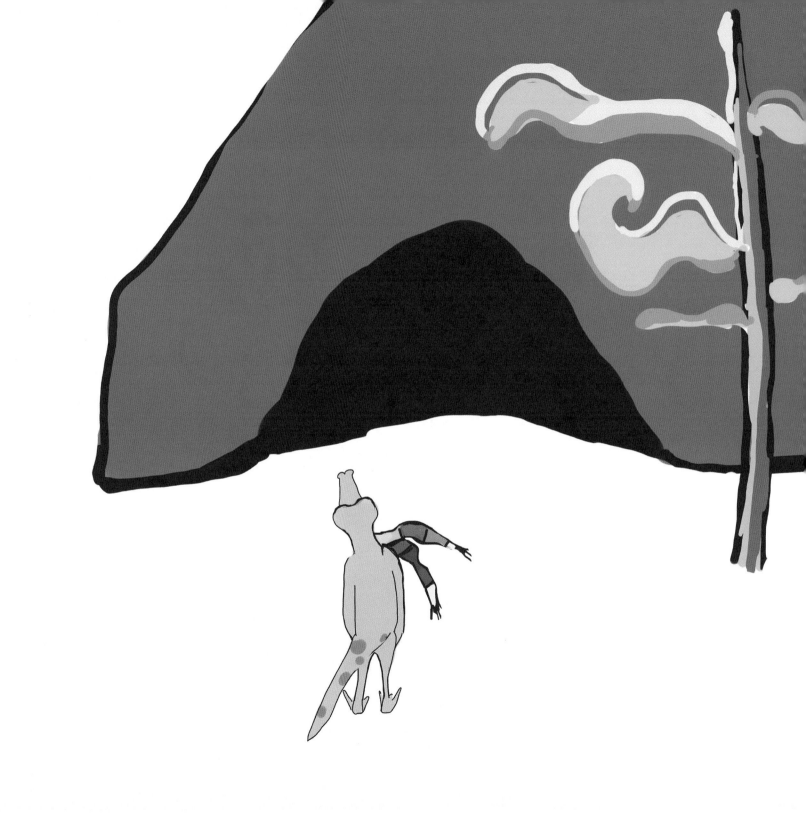

TIPS FOR DIFFUSING THE ALLIGATOR ON YOUR BACK

1. Always tell an adult how you're feeling: your parents, your teacher, or someone that you know cares about you. Talking about your feelings with an adult that cares about you is the best way to begin to get your alligator under control.
2. You are in charge of your alligator, and not the other way around.
3. Question all of your thoughts–especially ones that makes you feel sad, or unhappy. Ask yourself, is this me or my alligator talking to me? Is this thought serving me? Is this thought hurting me? Is this thought lifting me up and making me feel happy, or is it making me feel sad?
4. Diffuse your alligator's negative talk by:
   - Recognizing that it is coming from him and not you.
   - Asking him to please stop.
5. Diffuse his power by sharing your feelings and sending him to his cave.
6. GIVE YOURSELF A HUG every time you take charge of your alligator.
7. Make small positive changes in your thinking, every day.

More about the Alligator for Parents

In this story the alligator represents a deep sadness, or depression, that has climbed onto the boy's back.

Depression has an impact on a person's life. Depression is a type of mental illness that affects the way you feel, think, and act, just like the alligator affected the boy. Feelings of depression include feeling down, hopeless, and sad, and leave you unable to enjoy the things in life that you once did. Sometimes depression makes people feel hopeless, and also angry. Sometimes people with depression feel empty and numb. Depression in young people can be difficult to recognize. Many young people don't want to talk about their feelings or are unable to talk about them. Encouraging children to talk about their feelings is the most important step you can take. Listening is equally important. If you feel that your child may be depressed, please contact your doctor or local mental health association.

About the Author

Mary Ann Burrows is the author and illustrator of Gator on my Back. She was born and raised in the Fraser Valley in Chilliwack, B.C.

The mother of two adult children, she is an artist, a life/creativity coach, and the past founder of Artists in the Village Non-Profit Society. Mary Ann has a passion for creativity and children, and is dedicated to raising the awareness of mental health to reduce the stigma associated with mental illness.

Through her creativity she strives to help empower others, helping them rise to their own potential and live their happiest, healthiest lives. This is her second children's book. Her first book, Oh, Monkey! about the monkey-mind was released in the fall of 2019, and is available on www.ohmonkey.net.

A portion of every book sold is be donated to the Canadian Mental Health Association. CMHA provides advocacy, programs and resources that help to prevent mental health problems and illnesses, support recovery and resilience, and enable all Canadians to flourish and thrive.

CPSIA information can be obtained at www.ICGtesting.com
Printed in the USA
LVIW011725010520
653466LV00001BB/1